THREE
LITTLE PIGS

Illustrated by Daniel Howarth

sequoia™
children's publishing

Once upon a time, three little pigs decided to build themselves a house. But they could not agree on what kind of house to build.

In the end, they each built their own home. One was made of straw, one of sticks, and one of brick.

One day, the youngest pig heard a knock on
the door of his house made of straw. It was a wolf!
"Little pig, little pig, let me come in," he growled.
"Not by the hair of my chinny-chin-chin!" cried the pig.
"Then I'll huff, and I'll puff, and I'll blow your house
in!" the wolf yelled. And he did!
The little pig ran to his brother's house made of sticks.

Soon there was a knock on the door of the house
made of sticks. It was the wolf! "Little pigs, little pigs,
let me come in," he growled.

"Not by the hair of our chinny-chin-chins!" cried the pigs.

"Then I'll huff, and I'll puff, and I'll blow your house in!"
the wolf yelled. And he did!

The little pigs ran to their sister's house made of brick.

The wolf banged on the door of the house made of brick. "Little pigs, little pigs, let me come in," he growled.

"Not by the hair of our chinny-chin-chins!" cried the pigs.

"Then I'll huff, and I'll puff, and I'll blow your house in!" the wolf yelled.

He huffed and he puffed. He puffed and he huffed. But no matter how hard he blew, the house wouldn't budge!

Once more, the wolf knocked on the door.
"Little pigs!" he said sweetly. "Please let me come in."
"Not by the hair of our chinny-chin-chins!" called the pigs again.
"Then I'll find another way!" the wolf shouted.
The wolf looked up and saw the chimney.
He smiled to himself. He had an idea.

Suddenly, the pigs heard something on the roof.
They smiled to themselves. They had an idea, too.

The pigs quickly lit a fire in the fireplace. Just then,
the wolf dropped down through the chimney…and right
into the fire!

The wolf ran out the door, howling and fanning himself
as he went. The three little pigs waved merrily after him.

The three little pigs couldn't have been happier. The wolf never bothered them again. With their sister's help, the two little pigs rebuilt their houses in peace. Would it surprise you to learn that they were both made of brick?

ക്കൽ The End ക്കൽ

pig
(pigs)

Pigs are highly intelligent animals that live both on farms and in the wild. Although real pigs don't wear clothes, they do roll in mud to keep themselves cool and protect their skin. And while real pigs don't build houses, they do build nests to have babies and beds to rest in. People call pigs lazy, but wild pigs spend a lot of their time looking for food, playing, and even swimming. Does that sound lazy to you?

wolf
(wolves)

Wolves are large predators that can live almost anywhere, from the arctic to the desert. Wolves live far from people today, but in the past they lived much nearer. True to the story, wolves that lived too close to people often ate farm animals like pigs. People in turn hunted wolves to protect their farms. That's why there are not nearly as many wolves today as there used to be.

stick
(sticks)

Sticks are made of wood, of course, and wood is a common building material. Actual sticks are used in some places to build houses. The sticks are filled in with mud or clay for strength and insulation. The wooden house in the story is not very strong, but in the real world some wooden buildings are more than 1,000 years old. No wolf is going to blow them down!

brick
(bricks)

A **brick** is a rectangular block used in building. Bricks are made of things like clay or concrete and held together by a paste called mortar. True to the story, brick buildings are very strong. Some brick buildings are thousands and thousands of years old. Brick buildings are vulnerable to earthquakes. Maybe the wolf should have jumped and stomped instead of huffed and puffed!

straw
(straw)

Straw is what is left after you harvest a plant like wheat. It has a lot of uses, including bedding, weaving, and building. Straw is sometimes used to build the roof of a house. This is called a thatch roof. Whole houses aren't made of straw, but it is sometimes mixed with things like clay or concrete to make them stronger. Straw is transported in rectangular bundles called bales.

Story Discussion

After you are done reading the story, think about what each of the three pigs did with their houses and how they outsmarted the wolf. Be sure to look back at both the pictures and the words. Now it's time to answer these questions and talk about the story. After you read each question, choose the best answer or think of your own.

1.) In the beginning of the story, what big decision does each pig have to make?

What to eat for dinner.

What material to build their house with.

When to go to the store.

Something else?

2.) How do you think the three pigs felt inside the brick house?

They were worried the wolf would get in.

They were scared the house would fall down.

They felt safe behind the strong bricks.

Something else?

3.) At the end the wolf tried to come down the chimney of the brick house. What did the pigs do next?

They lit a fire in the fireplace.

They ran from the house.

They hid in the basement.

Something else?

4.) After reading about each of the pigs and their houses, what would you build your house out of?

Sticks

Brick

Straw

Something else?

Oh, no! The wolf is blowing the little pigs' house in! Can you spot 10 differences between the two pictures? (Answers on page 21)

Three Little Pigs follows a rule called The Rule of Three. This means things happen three at a time so they're easier to remember. There are three pigs and three houses. This exchange is repeated three times: "Little pig, little pig, let me come in." "Not by the hair of my chinny-chin-chin!" "Then I'll huff, and I'll puff, and I'll blow your house in!" Lots of stories and nursery rhymes use the rule of three. Some others are *Goldilocks and The Three Bears* and *Three Billy Goats Gruff*.

Three Little Pigs was first printed almost 200 years ago, but the story is much older than that. Before it was written down, people told the story to each other from memory. It was passed down from parents to children this way. This is called a folk tale.

Wolves in fairy tales often stand in for other dangerous parts of life. In *Three Little Pigs*, the wolf stands for unexpected things that can happen. This could be a bad storm that tries to blow your house down or a stranger who tries to talk you into opening your door.

Three Little Pigs is one of the most popular stories ever! It was one of the earliest fairy tales made into a cartoon. Plus, it has countless book versions, comic books, songs, movies, TV shows, and even video games based on it!